T0209382

HEAR MY CRY

CRY

TORKIKA TIBBS

BALBOA.PRESS

A DIVISION OF HAY HOUSE

This is a work of fiction. All of the characters, names, incidents,
organizations, and dialogue in this novel are either the products
of the author's imagination or are used fictitiously.

Balboa Press books may be ordered through booksellers or by contacting:

Balboa Press
A Division of Hay House
1663 Liberty Drive
Bloomington, IN 47403
www.balboapress.com
1 (877) 407-4847

Because of the dynamic nature of the Internet, any web addresses or
links contained in this book may have changed since publication and
may no longer be valid. The views expressed in this work are solely those
of the author and do not necessarily reflect the views of the publisher,
and the publisher hereby disclaims any responsibility for them.

The author of this book does not dispense medical advice or prescribe the use
of any technique as a form of treatment for physical, emotional, or medical
problems without the advice of a physician, either directly or indirectly. The
intent of the author is only to offer information of a general nature to help
you in your quest for emotional and spiritual well-being. In the event you use
any of the information in this book for yourself, which is your constitutional
right, the author and the publisher assume no responsibility for your actions.

Any people depicted in stock imagery provided by Getty Images are
models, and such images are being used for illustrative purposes only.
Certain stock imagery © Getty Images.

Print information available on the last page.

ISBN: 978-1-9822-4765-2 (sc)
ISBN: 978-1-9822-4766-9 (e)

Balboa Press rev. date: 05/14/2020

Don't cry mom, was the last words Angel heard her daughter say before she died. Angel never thought she would get the call from her daughter's principal saying that she was unresponsive and was being rushed to the hospital.

Aaliyah was a fourth grader at St. peters middle school in Baltimore, where she attended for five months. Not only was she new to the school but she also was new to the neighbor, so she didn't have any friends at all. After Aaliyah parents separated her and her mother packed up and moved from Florida, Aaliyah parents split up when she was only seven and it was hard for Aaliyah to cope with the fact of not having both parents and moving just made everything worse.

Aaliyah was at her school for a few months and she would come home crying everyday and when her mother would ask her what was bothering her, she would always say she was fine, and she did not want to talk about it. Angela thought maybe she was just still upset about the move and the fact that her farther was not there. Angela didn't seem to worry to much until Aaliyah stopped eating and stayed in her room every day after school.

You know maybe you should try and make some friends, Angela suggested.

I don't want any friends, Angela responded. Why did we even move here, I hate it here mom I don't want to go to school anymore, Aaliyah looked at her mother and began to cry, I want dad she screamed.

Angela did not know what to say at that moment, but she knew that something at school was bothering her and she knew she had to figure it out.

After a long night of screaming and crying Angela decided to go her daughter school to have lunch with her.

I will be at your school for lunch today Angela's said with a huge smile on her face.

Mom no! I will be fine Aaliyah said with this nervous look on her face, I will be ok.

Angel felt so helpless she knew something was bothering her daughter, but she did not want to invade her daughter's privacy.

As Aaliyah walked out the door, she turned around and said to her mother don't worry mom I will be ok.

Aaliyah came home that day with a smile on her face and kind of cheerful, so her mother thought maybe she had a good day at school. It was the next day May 3rd that changed Angels life for the worst, when she received the worst phone call about her daughter she was never expecting.

Mrs. Ford

Yes, this is Mrs. Ford.

This is Mr. Rogers the principal at St. peters middle school.

Is Aaliyah ok. Angel asked as she started to panic.

No Mrs. Ford there has been a accident and she is being rushed to memorial hospital, I suggest you have someone to drive you, before the principal could finish his conversation Angel dropped the phone grabbed her keys and ran out the her door.

Angel ran every light and stop sign trying to get to her daughter. She knew before her daughter went to school that something wasn't right.

Why Lord, why is this happening to me, Angel prayed all the way to the hospital. Lord please don't take my baby from me I need her Lord Amen. Angel had made it to the hospital where she seen the school nurse and the principal standing there nervously.

She looked at them both, where is my daughter, she screamed.

Mrs. Ford calm down please. Said the principal.

Before the principal could explain what happened the doctor came out.

What is going on with my daughter Angel asked the doctor.

Mrs. Ford Aaliyah suffered a lot of head trauma and has a lot of bleeding to her brain, explained the doctor.

Angel broke down.

Mrs. Ford Aaliyah was found by another student in the boy's bathroom unresponsive, the nurse explained, we did CPR we did what we could but there was still no response.

I can promise you that we will get to the bottom of this and take proper actions against whoever was involved.

I want to see my daughter now Angela screamed!

You can see her said the doctor, I just want you to know that she is in a coma and its not looking good.

Angel looked the doctors in the yes and said God has the final say so, now where is my daughter

The doctor escorted Angel to her daughters room, as Angel walked in her daughters room with tears running down her face, she could not believe she was next to her daughter in a hospital bed, she grabbed Aaliyah hand and begin to pray, Lord please protect my baby and bring her back to me, Amen.

Angel knew she had to be strong for her daughter, but all kinds of thoughts were running through her head. I should have gone to the school, I should have protected my baby, who would have done this to my daughter is all she could think about. She could not understand why her daughter didn't tell her about any problems that she was having in school.

Angel had learned from the investigator that Aaliyah was being picked on every day, beaten and called names, and she didn't eat lunch because she had her money taken.

Angel thought Aaliyah was doing so good, she was so excited about making the basketball team, and every time she asked her about school, she would tell her not to worry that everything was ok. She didn't understand why someone would hurt her daughter.

Angel never left her daughter side she set for hours by her side just thinking how could she let her daughter down she did not deserve Angel said as she started to cry, was is because she was black, or smart or beautiful, she needed answers. She knew Mr. Fords voice, so she didn't have to turn around.

I came as fast as I could cried Mr. Ford, he went to his daughter side, how could this happen to her, she didn't deserve this.

I don't know what happen to my baby cried Angel, I should have been there to protect her.

Its not your fault Angel, said Mr. Ford as he walked over to hug her, everything will be ok.

Angel hugged Mr. Ford tight and started to cry harder. Why would someone want to hurt, she didn't do anything to anybody she is a good kid.

I know angel but we must stay calm, Mr. Ford knew that Angel was not listening.

Stay calm, how dare you tell me to stay calm and our daughter is laying in a hospital bed almost dead. I will not calm down until I find out what happened to my daughter.

Look said Mr. Ford, she is my daughter too and I want to find out what happen to her just as bad as you do, but us screaming and fighting will not get us anywhere.

As much as Angel did not want to hear Mr. Ford, she knew that he was right, but it wasn't enough for her.

Why don't you go home shower and get some rest and I will stay here until you get back, Mr. Ford suggested.

Angel didn't want to leave her daughter side, but she knew she needed rest.

Ok! she responded but I will be back in two hours.

It was so hard for Mr. Ford to see his daughter so helpless; he took her hand and begin to talk and pray. Lord I need you right now to heal my daughter just keep your protecting arms around her Amen.

Mr. Ford wiped his tears and started to talk to his daughter, I need you baby please don't give up on me, we will find out what happen to you I promise.

Angel had a lot on her mind she knew she wouldn't be able to rest so she decided to shower and head to the school to do her own investigation. Angel had a lot to deal with she did not let the fact that she found out she had stage three breast cancer get in the way of finding out what happened to her daughter. Angel found out she had breast cancer four months ago and she didn't know how to tell her husband or her daughter. She wore wigs to cover her hair lost and she is so strong that nobody even knew she was sick most of the time.

When Angel walked into the school all the students gave her a look like she had no business being there, she noticed that there was only a few African American students there and they all looked terrified and she knew right then that her daughter had suffered a lot of abuse and was scare to tell her.

How is Aaliyah doing, asked the principal, I heard she wasn't doing to good

Mr. rogers I need to know what happened to my daughter, someone seen something heard something I need to know, please just help me cried Angela.

Look Mrs. Ford said the principal I want to help you I really do, and I am truly sorry about what happened to your daughter, but I can not give you any information on a case that is still under investigation. The police have all the camera footage and all the evidence they need, there is nothing more that I can do or say at this moment.

Mr. Rogers do u have children asked Angel.

I have two Mr. Rogers responded.

If you were in my shoes would you fight for your kids, would you be able to sleep at night knowing someone has harmed your child and they are fighting for their life. Well guess what Angel screamed I will fight for my daughter; I will find out who did to her and I will get justice for her.

Again, I am very sorry Mrs. ford. Before he could finish Angel turned around and stormed out the door, she noticed as she walked out that the students were looking at her and laughing, she continued to walk when she realized that her daughter locker was destroyed someone had wrote things like fight harder next time, and you won't make it.

Angel turned around to the principal what type of principal are you, you allow this type of behavior in your school. Angel broke down as she left the school, she couldn't believe what type of things were wrote on her daughter locker.

May 8th 2002 Aaliyah was taken of life support she had been in a coma for weeks, no movements or anything and Angel and Mr. Ford didn't want Aaliyah to suffer anymore, they knew it was time to let her go. Aaliyah being there 0nly child was so hard for them, they knew that God had other plans for their daughter, but they also knew that they had to really find out what happened to their daughter.

It was going to be a busy week for the Fords they felt so alone like no one was there for them they felt if everyone was against them, but they weren't going to let that stop them from finding out what happened to their daughter. The hardest part was planning a funeral.

We must stay strong cried Mr. Ford.

I don't know how much I can take cried Angela, everything is happening to fast.

Everything will be ok replied Mr. Ford.

Its not going to be ok yelled Angela, you know why because my daughter is gone, I have cancer and the doctors are only giving me four months to live.

Are you serious, why wouldn't you tell me, cried Mr. Ford how long has this been going on.

I don't want to talk about it, I just want it all to be over with Angel replied.

As Angel and Mr. Ford were leaving the hospital, they heard a lot of noises saying No Justice No peace, they noticed that there were hundredths of people outside the hospital supporting them, and not only that the principal even came to help to. Angela knew that the talk she had with the principal had worked.

Angela and Mr. Ford knew they still had to focus on who murdered their daughter and plan for a funeral as well.

Look said Mr. Ford, I will stay as long as you need me to Angel. I know things are tight for you and I will be willing to help as much as I can.

I will be fine Angela responded, you have your own life and I will not get in the way of that.

Angel none of that matters, what matters right now is you and my daughter and getting justice for her.

As angel started to walk away Mr. Ford gently grabbed her arm.

Look I know we may have had our differences and I have not been here like I should have but I am here now, and we have to pull together for Aaliyah.

Angel knew she needed the money and extra help she was fired when Aaliyah was hospitalized, and she has been very sick.

Ok you can stay, but only a month I will find another job and get back

On my feet and you can get back to your life. You can stay in the guest room, everything u need will be in there.

Thank You Angel, said Mr. Ford.

Angel and Mr. Ford had already notified their families, and as they prepare for the every ones arrival they knew they had to answer other questions about them being separated, and they still have not gotten any answers on what happened to Aaliyah, they have called their lawyers and the investigators still no answers.

Two days before the funeral Angela got a call from a parent of a student who attended school with Aaliyah.

Mrs. Ford my name is Samantha Peterson my son attended school with your daughter, is there any way we can meet Samantha asked.

Angel begin to shake as she gave Samantha her address, she felt like she had gotten a little closer to finding out what happened to her daughter.

Thank you, Lord, cried Angel you have answered my prayers.

Samantha and her son had arrived.

We are so sorry for your lost cried Samantha as she hugged Angel. We want to help in any way that we can.

Thank you replied Angela.

My son has information that I think would be helpful and may ease some pain.

Tell her Daniel its ok. Daniel looked so nervous, as he began to talk.

I was in the bathroom when Aaliyah was attacked, I was hiding in the bathroom when I heard, Daniel paused.

Its ok said Angel.

Daniel continued, I was hiding when I heard Josh and Amanda attacking her in the boys bathroom, I was so scared, they covered her mouth so she screamed, they punched and slapped her so many times, Daniel started to cry, they even banged her head so many times, all you seen was blood and that's when I dropped my books in the stool and that's when the attacked stopped, they made me open the door and dragged me out and told me if I told anyone they would kill me.

I am so sorry said Daniel I wanted to help her, but I was so scared.

Angel couldn't listen anymore, she got up and walked away she couldn't listen to all the things her daughter went through all the pain she just didn't understand why someone could be so harsh.

Was my daughter still alive when you left the bathroom.

She was not moving or anything, she was bleeding from her head and ears said Daniel. When I seen Josh and Amanda run out the bathroom is when I ran and got the principal, and all I see was them taking her to the ambulance.

All Mr. Ford could do was put his head down and cry, thank you guys for all your help.

As Samantha and her son were leaving, she turned around and said Mr. and Mrs. Ford I am really sorry for your lost and no matter what we will always be here for you guys.

Angel went and cuddled in Aaliyah bed and cried until she fell asleep.

Mr. Ford went to check on her, he seen that she was sleep so he started to walk out the room.

She was a good girl Angel started to talk, she did not deserve what she went through, I know she suffered and I know she put up a good fight, I know she would want us to be strong and fight until we get justice.

Are you going to be ok Angel, Mr. Ford asked Angel our daughter was very strong, and I know she will be looking down on us making sure we are ok, and we will fight until we get justice for our baby.

The day had come for everyone to say their last goodbyes and as hard as it was for Angel and Mr. Ford they had a lot of support from family and friends there were people who didn't know Aaliyah but heard about what happened that were there. Aaliyah funeral was so beautiful there were all kinds of pictures of Aaliyah smiling and being a normal kid people from all over had heard Aaliyah story and pitched in and helped with the funeral they mad her casket barbies because that's what she liked. It was such a beautiful homegoing.

It was time for Angel to speak and she knew she had to very strong no matter how much it hurt. Angel message was pointing towards all children she wanted them to know that bullying was not ok and that if they were going through it or know someone who is they need talk to someone and don't be afraid.

Always believe in yourself said Angel, you have the right to stand up for yourself, never be afraid to speak out and let someoneknow when you are being bullied or know someone who is being bullied. Bullying is not ok I lost my daughter to bullying I will never be able to see her again, my daughter was very strong and brave, and if I can prevent this from happening to someone else I will. Angel knew that her daughter was proud of her and she knew she was smiling down oh her.

A day after the funeral Angel and Mr. Ford got the phone call they were waiting for the cameras were viewed and it showed a girl and a boy dragging Aaliyah into the boys bathroom and it also showed Daniel running out and the two students running out shortly after him.

So, what's going to happen to these kids asked Mr. Ford.

We must have physical evidence a witness we have to have more said the investigator they have been placed on suspension until further noticed.

Suspension, these kids brutally attacked my daughter and killed her and all they get is suspension.

Mr. Ford we are doing everything we can to find out what happened to your daughter.

No, you're not cried Angela, its cause she's black that nothing matters.

Calm down Angela said Mr. Ford.

No, I'm not going to calm down until justice is served.

Look Mrs. Ford I understand exactly what you are going through said the detective we will need physical evidence or witnesses someone who saw something, and we can put these students away for murder.

Angel and Mr. Ford knew they had to get Samantha's son to testify and they knew it wasn't going to be easy, but it was worth the try. They went to Samantha's house to try and talk them into letting their son testify.

Look said Samantha, this is a big step. Is he going to have to testify in front of the people who hurt Aaliyah?

Yes, but I guarantee everything will be ok.

I don't know said Samantha.

I'm not scared said Samantha's son, I want to do it, I want to do this for Aaliyah.

Angela started to smile as tears ran down her eyes.

Samantha decided to let her son testify. Ok so what do we do now.

Its going to be a hard case to beat but if we stick to the truth, we will be ok explained Angela.

It was June 3rd time for court and Mr. Ford and Angela was so nervous, seeing that these two kids have rich parents and lawyers they didn't think they could stand a chance on winning.

Why are they smiling, Angela felt herself ready to explode, as the students that murdered her daughter was brought in smiling.

Angela calm down we must stay calm said Mr. Ford.

Angela stayed calm as everyone spoke. It was time for the verdict.

All rise said the bailiff. Have the jury reached a verdict.

We the jury find the defendants Guilty.

Angela started to cry and they both felt so relieved even though they were not found guilty of murder, but they were found guilty of manslaughter there was some type of justice for Aaliyah.

Angela could think Samantha and her son because of him being so strong justice was served.

It was the day of sentencing and Angela and Mr. Ford was hoping for great news, but when they heard that the students were only going to serve fifteen years things got out of hand.

Fifteen years shouted Angela, that's not enough.

Order in the court repeated the judge.

They murdered my daughter, Angela had to be escorted out the court room on her way out she shouted murder. She felt like the justice system failed her daughter and she didn't know how to handle it.

It was time for Angela to take the stand.

My daughter didn't deserve this she didn't deserve to be beat. She was smart, she loved to play basketball, and she loved to swim, she went on to say my daughter is not a troublemaker, I won't be able to see my daughter hug or kiss her anymore. What did she do to you Angela asked Amanda and Josh.

It was so hard for Angel to get up and talk in front of her daughter's killer, but she did it and now that she has her closure, she can have peace now.

It wasn't a day that went by that Angela didn't go visit Aaliyah's grave Angela have been sick dealing with cancer, but she didn't let that stop her she would just sit there and talk to her daughter for hours, I love you baby girl and no matter what I will always keep your name alive.

Every year on Aaliyah's birthday her and Aaliyah would have special cupcakes so she continued the trend she would eat two cupcakes one for her and one for Aaliyah.

What do we do from here asked Mr. Ford, I had dreams for all of us, and now there gone the death of Aaliyah and Angela being sick is really hitting him hard he tried to be strong for the family but he knew and felt like he was losing it.

Look said Angela it's a tough time for us both, and it's going to take time for us to heal but right now I just need time to heal and get well. Angela was trying to be strong even though her body was in a lot of pain, I just need to be alone to think and figure out what I am going to do from here.

What about work and bills asked Mr. Ford, how will you get by.

I will be fine I already been offered three jobs working with kids at schools and being a speaker about bullying, so I am sure I will be fine.

You can barely stand up how will you be fine Angela just let me stay and help you. Suggested Mr. Ford.

Look just go and get back to your life I will make it with God on my side everything will be ok.

Mr. Ford hugged Angela; I love you Angela he said. I will go pack just know if you ever need me, I am just a phone call away.

I know responded Angela and Thank you for just being here, that means a lot to me. Angela knew she was going to feel alone but she knew she had to get on with her life and do what was important to her. Angela was fighting cancer she was sick every day, and she knew her time was coming to a end but she didn't let that stop her from doing what she wanted to do and that was helping children who was being bullied and couldn't open up about it, she wanted to help children all over the world she did speeches on bullying she wrote books that's she had dedicated to Aaliyah.

Aaliyah message was very powerful everyone wanted her to speak at conferences full of children that she knew were being bullied but could not open up about it.

Angela was so proud of her accomplishments and she knew that Aaliyah would be proud, she knew her daughter was smiling down on her Angela touched hearts everywhere children, elderly people and adults, there wasn't anyone who didn't love Angela she helped young people find their self she helped them open up and not be afraid to stand up and tell someone if they are being bullied or know someone who is being bullied.

Angela had a message for all the children around the world.

No matter what obstacles you may face in life always open up, you are not alone someone hears your cry, bullying is not ok if you are experiencing it or see it don't be afraid to tell someone you can save your life as well as someone else. Let's stick together and stop bullying.

Angela loved what she do but she knew it was coming to a end, she was really sick and the doctor only gave her a few weeks to live, Angela was going through chemo the cancer had come back and had traveled through her body. Angela never thought her one and only child would die before her and she never thought that she would have to deal with cancer at the age of forty, she kept it from her husband and her daughter and now she cant even tell her daughter.

Angela was on her last days and Mr. Ford rushed back to be by her side.

People that supported Angela was by her side they sent flowers and cards and some even came to visit her the, everyone was so sad to hear the news that one of their inspirational people were dying.

On July tenth Angela had passed away and it hurt everyone across the world everyone knew Angela from helping them stand up for themselves and stand up to bullies.

Mr. ford life was turned upside down he lost two of the most important people in his life, he always told Angela she needed to be strong, but he tried to take his own advice which was hard, he cried everyday and felt like he couldn't live anymore.

Angela funeral was so beautiful it even made the news all over people from all over had come out to the funeral there were a lot of candles and tears shared for Angela, she looked so beautiful and peaceful and they buried her right next to her Aaliyah.

Angela was so strong, and she didn't stop until her message was clear to everyone around the world and she succeeded, and she will always be remembered.

I was inspired to write this book because bullying is happening every day, 20 percent of student are being bullied every day and that's to many. We must speak up and let our children know that bullying is not ok its not ok to bully or be bullied. Its ok to talk to someone and let them know what's going on. If you feel like no one is listening talk to someone else until they listen.

This book is so important to me I was bullied when I was in elementary, I couldn't open up to anyone about it because I was afraid I was teased, beat, and I was also chased home, I wrote this book to let others know they don't have to deal with being bullied.

Printed in the United States
By Bookmasters